STA[N] SAVES THE AMAZON RAINFOREST

BY

TONY FRAIS

Tony Frais

Illustrations by Rosalind Wilson

Published in 2008 by ANTHONY T. FRAIS,
9 Sandhill Oval, LEEDS LS17 8EB
UNITED   KINGDOM
afrais@tiscali.co.uk

ISBN 13   978 0 9548068 2 8

INTRODUCTION

WHO IS STANLEY THE SPIDER?

Stanley the spider made his first appearance in Tony Frais' first book 'Noah's Rocket'.
Stanley was living in the Amazon Rainforest when he was taken away by men who were capturing creatures to be sold on the 'Largest Pet Shop in the World' website.
On the other side of the world, a huge flood was coming and a man called Noah had been instructed to build a giant space rocket to take

himself, his family and two of every kind of living thing into the rocket and blast off into space and go into orbit around the Earth until it was safe to return. Noah had ordered a male and female of all the creatures from the 'Largest Pet Shop in the World.'

Stanley the spider was one of those creatures.

With the rocket in orbit, Noah had decided to send a spider spinning down to Earth in order to find an object to take back to the rocket to show the flood had gone.

Stanley bravely volunteered for the mission.

Wearing a protective red woolly space suit specially knitted for him by Noah's wife, Stanley set off on his mission down to Earth.

In the next book 'Stanley's Space Adventure', Stanley was selected to go back into space to explore the mysterious planets of Fruton and Vegeton.

After successfully solving the mystery of how fruit and vegetables came to inhabit these strange and distant planets, Stanley was flying back to Earth, when he spotted his home in the Amazon Rainforest from space. Stanley began to feel homesick and decided that he wanted to go home.

Arriving back on Earth, Stanley asked the scientists who had sent him on his mission if he could use the rocket to get back home and the scientists agreed. Stanley

blasted off to return to the
Rainforest.

However, there was one small
mystery that Stanley had not
solved. Someone had given him
the gift of a teapot to take with him
on his space mission. Stanley
could not understand what the
teapot could be used for but it was
still in the rocket as he flew home.

CHAPTER 1

Stanley's rocket was approaching his home in the Amazon Rainforest. He steered the rocket downwards and prepared for landing. Stanley touched down and in seconds, a large crowd of curious creatures made their way to where the rocket had landed. Still wearing his red woolly space suit, Stanley opened the door of the rocket and climbed out. He was so happy to see his Rainforest friends once again and was sure that they would all remember him.
 One of the ants walked towards Stanley.
 "Who are you and what are you?" said the ant.

"I'm Stanley spider. Don't you remember me?"

"Hang on a minute," said the ant. "You look like a spider but I don't remember any spider living in this Rainforest who wears a red woolly suit!"

Stanley thought he should take off his suit so that everyone would recognize him.

"It *is* Stanley!" shouted the ant. "Look everybody!"

The other creatures cheered and clapped.

"Welcome home Stanley. We thought we would never see you again!" said the ant.

"It's great to be back home to see you all again!" said Stanley.

"So what's the red woolly suit all about?" asked the ant.

Stanley told him that when he went on his space missions, he needed to wear a protective red woolly space suit and that he liked it so much, he decided to wear it all the time!

"So what did you do on your trips into space Stanley?" asked the ant. Stanley told them all about his adventures and what he'd achieved.

The creatures were fascinated by Stanley's stories.

"Yes it was exciting and sometimes a bit scary, but enough of my stories. How are things in the Rainforest these days?" asked Stanley.

The ant spoke up: "To tell you the truth Stanley, things are not too good at the moment.

King of the Rainforest, Jaguar, isn't well at the moment and he's feeling very sad. He's not patrolling the forest as he usually does, keeping things under control. Some of the monkeys have started to take advantage of this and are making a lot of trouble.

They've started throwing stones at us for fun and it's become dangerous walking around the Rainforest, because you never know when you are going to get hit by one. A stick insect had a stone land right on top of his head and he was out of action for three weeks. On top of all that, we have another serious problem. Men are coming into the Rainforest and they are chopping down lots of trees. If this goes on there will be no Rainforest left and where are we all going to live if that happens?"

"I'm very sorry to hear all this bad news," said Stanley. "Perhaps the King will get better soon and start sorting out these problems but it's still good to be back home and now, if you don't mind, I'm going to put my suit back on."

"That's a good idea Stanley," said the ant. "I'll let all the Rainforest creatures know you're back and if they want to find you I'll tell them to look out for a red woolly spider!"

CHAPTER 2

Stanley put his red woolly suit
back on and turned to shut the door
of the rocket when he spotted the
teapot.

"Might as well clean up the rocket
and throw out that teapot," thought
Stanley. He took the teapot out of
the rocket but as he did so, the lid
dropped off and four pieces of
paper fell out.

"Well I never thought to look and
see what was inside the teapot!"
thought Stanley.

Picking up the pieces of paper he
noticed that there was some
writing on them. The first paper
said: *Instructions for making an
electric guitar.* The second paper
said: *How to play the electric*

guitar. The third paper said: *How to make a guitar amplifier.* Finally, the fourth paper said: *How to play the teapot.*

He showed the instructions to the ant.

"What do you make of this?" asked Stanley.

"Very unusual. Can't see why someone would want you to make and play an electric guitar or learn how to play a teapot," replied the ant.

"Maybe someone wanted me to have something to do while I was on my mission to explore the distant planets, but I didn't have any of things you need to make a guitar on board the rocket and, as for playing the teapot, that doesn't sound very interesting, apart from blowing down the spout to make it sound like a trumpet!" said Stanley.

Looking at the instructions again, the ant pointed out to Stanley that the wood he needed to build the guitar and the amplifier could be cut from a fallen branch.

"Well that's a start," said Stanley. "But the instructions also say that you need a power supply for the amplifier and there's no electricity in the middle of the Rainforest is there?"

"Well that's that!" said the ant.

Stanley suddenly remembered something.

"Before I was captured and taken away from the Rainforest, I remember talking to a frog, who knew an alligator, who had heard

from a fish about a weird sort of
eel living in the Amazon River that
produces electricity. One of these
eels had got hold of a light bulb
that was dropped from a boat
going down the river. When the eel
touched the bottom of the light
bulb it would light up!
Now that's the story as I remember
it and that's how I could get my
supply of electricity! I must get
down to the river and see if I can
find one of these electric eels."
Stanley put the instructions back
inside the teapot and made his way
to the river bank.
After a while, he spotted an
alligator swimming down the river.
Stanley called out to say that he
wanted a word and the alligator

swam towards the river bank
where Stanley was sitting.
"Hello Stanley spider," said the
alligator. "Just got the news that
you were back in the Rainforest.
What can I do for you?"
Stanley asked him if he could find
an electric eel because he wanted
to ask him something.
"I'll go and get one for you if you
like," said the alligator. The
alligator swam off and returned
with an electric eel swimming
beside him. The eel spoke from
under the water.
"Hebbo, hy hab han hebectric
heel."
"What did he say?" asked Stanley.
The alligator explained that when
the eel talks underwater, it's

difficult to understand what he's saying!

The alligator dipped his head into the water and had a word with the eel, who popped his head out of the water and introduced himself again.

"Hello, I am an electric eel."

Stanley explained to the eel about needing him as a supply of electricity to power a guitar amplifier.

"No problem," said the eel. "I've got lots of electricity to spare, so happy to help. Just come back to the river whenever you need me."

CHAPTER 3

Stanley thanked the eel and made his way back to where he had left the teapot with the instructions inside. He took the pieces of paper out and began reading them.

"Hi Stanley!" said a lizard who was passing by. "What are you reading?"

"It's instructions on how to build an electric guitar and an amplifier," replied Stanley.

"Wow, that sounds really cool!" said the lizard. "I'll give you a hand if you like."

Stanley and the lizard read the first instruction.

First build the body of the guitar. Cut out a flat piece of wood; draw the shape of the guitar onto the

18

wood and then cut around the shape.

"Well there's a problem straight away", said Stanley. "What do I use to cut out a piece of wood?" The lizard had to think about this but then he said: "A good friend of mine is a piranha fish. He's got really sharp teeth, so he could cut out the wood for you and when you've drawn the shape of the guitar onto the wood, he could cut that out as well. Not only that, but he could also cut the wood you need to build the amplifier!"

"Sounds like a great idea," said Stanley. "Let's go and find your friend."

"OK Stanley," said the lizard. "But we'll need something that we can fill with water so we can carry him around."

Stanley and the lizard had a look around the Rainforest floor to find something that would hold water when the lizard spotted a small hollow log.

"Perfect!" said Stanley.

The next task for Stanley and the lizard was to go down to the river and try and persuade the piranha to help them. Reaching the river, the lizard shouted out "PIRANHA, PIRANHA!" A piranha popped his head out of the water and the lizard asked if he could help with cutting some wood.

"That is a very unusual job for a fish but I'd be happy to help," said the piranha.

Stanley lifted the piranha out of the river and gently dropped him into the hollow log. When that was done, they made their way back into the Rainforest.

"Here's a fallen branch from a Rosewood tree, Stanley. Let's use this one!" said the lizard.

Stanley took the piranha out of the log, held him by his tail and told him to get his teeth going to cut a piece of wood from the branch.

The next sound heard was the fast *chomp, chomp, chomp,* of the piranha's teeth as it cut out a flat piece of wood.

"Like to take a breather now if you don't mind," said the piranha. Stanley put the fish back into the log.

Next, using a sharp stone, Stanley drew the shape of the guitar onto the wood. He took the piranha out of the log and guided its cutting teeth around the shape of the guitar.

"Brilliant!" said Stanley. "Now I've got the guitar body, let's cut the wood for the amplifier."

After that was done, the lizard offered to take the piranha back to the river. Stanley thanked the piranha and the lizard for their help and then read the next instruction.

Put six strings onto the guitar.

"Here's another problem," thought Stanley. "What am I going to use for strings?"

Just then, the ant happened to be walking by.

"Hello ant," said Stanley.

"Hello Stanley, how's things?" replied the ant.

Stanley asked where he could find any metal wire.

"Not far from here Stanley. Men who come into the Rainforest leave all sorts of things behind," said the ant.

Stanley explained he needed pieces of wire not only to connect the electric eel to the amplifier and his guitar to the amplifier but also he needed the wire to make the strings for the guitar.

"No problem!" said the ant. "I'll go and fetch the wire for you."

After a short while, the ant came back with a bundle of wire.

Stanley selected the right lengths of wire for the strings and fixed them on the guitar.

"Going to be a rock'n'roll star Stanley?" asked the ant.

"Not really, it's just for a bit of fun and entertainment," said Stanley.

"OK, see you around," said the ant.

The ant marched off and Stanley sat down and started reading the instructions on how to play the electric guitar.

CHAPTER 4

Day after day, Stanley practised playing his guitar and the more he practised, the better he got. In between practising, he began work on building the amplifier.

The ant came to see how he was getting on.

"Sounds like you are going to be a great guitarist Stanley. I can just about hear what you're playing without using the amplifier."

"Thanks," said Stanley. "But what I really want to do now is plug the guitar into the amplifier and really let rip!"

Just then, a lady spider walked past where Stanley was practising. She stopped and took a good look at Stanley and said: "I know you!

You're Stanley! I've heard you were back in the Rainforest and were wearing a red woolly suit!" Stanley remembered the lady spider, put his guitar down and gave her a big eight-legged hug. "Good to see you again lady spider. What have you been up to whilst I've been away?"

"It's a long story Stanley, but I got married last year."

"Congratulations!" said Stanley. "Any kids yet?"

"Sure," said the lady spider. "I've had a few thousand so far; in fact my latest five hundred are still very young. They're playing together in that clearing over there. Actually Stanley, could you do me a favour? My husband usually looks after them for me but he has gone off with his tarantula friend to see the carnival in Rio de Janeiro. I've got to go out and catch some flies to feed the kids. Could you watch over them until I get back?"

"OK," said Stanley.

He decided to take his guitar with him and headed towards the clearing where all the spider kids were. He sat down, and in between looking to see that the kids were alright, he practised playing. Eventually, the lady spider returned with food for her kids. "Thanks Stanley, do you think you could do this for me again tomorrow?"

"Will do," said Stanley.

As Stanley walked away, he thought of a great idea. "I could set the amplifier up in the clearing and try out my guitar!"

The next day, Stanley picked up the hollow log and made his way down to the river.

Stanley called out: "ELECTRIC EEL, ELECTRIC EEL!"

The eel popped his head out of the water.

"Hi Stanley, what's up?"

"Please could you power my guitar amplifier?" asked Stanley.

"OK Stanley, no problem," said the eel.

Stanley lifted the eel out of the river and dropped him into the log. He made his way back through the Rainforest to the clearing where the lady spider was waiting for him to look after the kids again.

"Morning Stanley," she said.

"Thanks for doing this again. What's with the eel?"

Stanley explained. He then went back to pick up his guitar and the amplifier and took them to the clearing.

"OK Stanley, I'm off. See you in a bit," said the lady spider.

Stanley attached a piece of wire around the eel's body and plugged the other end into the amplifier. Then he fixed another piece of wire into the guitar and plugged that into the amplifier.
All that was left to do was turn the amplifier on.

CHAPTER 5

Stanley flicked the amplifier's 'on' switch and turned the volume knob up to maximum. Stanley began playing his guitar.

The noise was just fantastic! All the spider kids stopped playing and began to listen to a sound they had never heard before. It was not long before they were bouncing up and down to Stanley's guitar playing.

It wasn't only the spider kids who heard Stanley playing. For miles around the Rainforest, all the creatures had also heard Stanley's guitar. Most of them wanted to see what was going on, so they made their way over to the clearing where the sound was coming from.

Before long, hundreds of the Rainforest's creatures had come to see and hear Stanley playing. Shortly after all this was happening, the lady spider returned.

"What is going on here?" she asked a dancing chameleon.

"That spider is a really cool guitar player, don't you think?" said the chameleon.

The lady spider was not impressed. She went over to where Stanley was still giving everything he'd got on his guitar and turned off the amplifier. Everybody booed the lady spider for doing that.

"What do you think you're playing at Stanley?" she said. "I leave you alone to look after my kids, I come

back and the whole place is packed
with wild dancing creatures!"
"Sorry about that," said Stanley.
"I'll tell them the recital is over."
Stanley shouted out: "OK folks,
that's it for now. Hope you
enjoyed the guitar playing."
All the creatures cheered and
clapped then made their way back
into the Rainforest.
"Anyway, thanks Stanley," said
the lady spider. "I'll see you
tomorrow, only don't play so
loudly!"
Stanley disconnected the wire from
the eel to the amplifier and made
his way back to the river.
"Great music," said the eel. "It was
so loud, I could hear everything,
even when I was underwater!"

"Thanks," said Stanley. He tipped the eel back into the river.

"Use me again, anytime you like. See you Stanley," said the eel.

CHAPTER 6

At the palace of Jaguar, King of the Rainforest, things were not getting any better. The King was still not feeling very well – in fact he was getting worse and was not interested in doing what a King needs to do.

His advisors had told him that the monkeys of the Rainforest had started to run wild and were throwing stones at the other creatures. There were also rumours that trees were being chopped down by men coming in to the Rainforest.

But King Jaguar was not interested. All he would say was: "Leave me alone, I really couldn't care less."

The King's advisors were getting more and more upset about the situation.
They wondered what to do next in order to make the King happy again so he could go back to patrolling the Rainforest. An iguana advisor came up with an idea.

"A few days ago, I was on my way back to the palace when I heard the sound of music coming from a clearing in the Rainforest. When I got there, there was a spider wearing a red woolly suit playing a guitar very loudly. Everyone there was jumping around to the music and they all seemed to be having a good time. I wonder if we should ask this spider if he would come to the palace with his guitar and play for the King. It might cheer him up and make him feel better."

"Why not?" said a frog advisor. "May as well try it. What have we got to lose? Go and find this spider!"

The iguana agreed that he would go and ask the spider if he would come to the palace and play for the King.

The next morning, Stanley picked up the eel and turned up to look after the spider kids and play his guitar.

The iguana walked into the clearing where Stanley was playing and stood waving one of his legs in front of him.

Stanley stopped playing.

"Now then iguana, what can I do for you today?" asked Stanley.

"Mr. Spider, I suppose you have heard that King Jaguar is not well at the moment. I was wondering whether you would like to come and play for him because it might just cheer him up."

"I'd be happy to," said Stanley.
"As soon as the lady spider comes
back, I can come along."
Just then, the lady spider returned.
 "Right," said Stanley to the
iguana. "Let's go to the palace.
Please could you give me a hand to
carry all the stuff over?"
The iguana picked up the
amplifier. Stanley picked up his
guitar and the eel.
"Playing somewhere else now?"
asked the eel.
"Yes," replied Stanley. "We are
going to the palace to play for the
King." The eel was very
impressed. "Playing at the palace
for the King! Wow, that really is
something special!"
They all set off for the palace.
Once there, Stanley was shown

into a large hall. "You can set up here," said the iguana. "I'll go and get the King."

Stanley got everything ready. The King arrived in the hall and sat down on a chair. Stanley introduced himself.

"Hello King Jaguar. I am Stanley and I have come here today to play for you."

Stanley began playing his guitar at full volume.

Within seconds, the King was up on his feet, jumping up and down and enjoying every minute of Stanley's performance.

The iguana was overjoyed to see the King in such high spirits once again.

Stanley played on until the King raised his paw.

"Well done Stanley!" said the King. "You have made me happy again!"

Stanley told him that the Rainforest creatures would be thrilled to hear that their King was well again. He also asked if he knew of the problems that were threatening the Rainforest. The King spoke:

"I have heard about the monkeys running riot and a new rumour that they want to take over the Rainforest as well, so I must try to sort this out. I have also heard about the tree choppers and that is by far the most serious problem. I always listen to what my advisors have to say but they have yet to come up with any solutions. Perhaps you could help me with these problems Stanley? I'll meet you at your place tomorrow morning and we'll talk about what can be done."

CHAPTER 7

The next morning, the King came
along to see Stanley.
At the same time and just a short
distance away, a lot of monkeys
had gathered together. On seeing
the King, they shouted out to him.
"We see you are back again King
Jaguar but we are now set to
become Kings of the Rainforest
and we plan to attack you and the
rest of the creatures."
The King had to think very quickly
what to do about the threatened
attack. But whilst he was thinking,
a giant monkey shouted over to
him.
"Instead of a war between us, send
out one of your creatures to fight

me in a boxing match. The winner
will be the King of the Rainforest."
 Stanley spoke up:
"Let me take on the giant monkey,
I think I could win!"
Although it seemed to the King
that Stanley was too small to take
on and beat the giant monkey, he
decided that the fight should go
ahead because he thought that
Stanley knew exactly what he was
doing.
The King shouted back to the giant
monkey.
"We agree. The winner of the
boxing match becomes King of the
Rainforest. How about nine o'
clock tomorrow night in the forest
clearing?"

The giant monkey shouted back. "We agree. Who will be representing you?"

"Stanley the spider," replied the King.

The monkey went straight back to his friends to tell them the news that the opposition was putting up a spider to fight him. On hearing this, all the monkeys just fell about laughing. One of them said:

"Fancy putting up a little spider to fight you! Looks like this time tomorrow we will be the Kings of the Rainforest!"

Meanwhile, King Jaguar was very concerned that Stanley could be easily beaten by the giant monkey.

"Stanley, I am very worried that you may be the tragic hero by getting squashed in the first round.

That will do none of us any good,"
said the King.

But Stanley had a secret plan.

"Don't worry," said Stanley. "I
won't let you down. I'll beat that
giant monkey."

"Right," said the King. "First thing
is to make a boxing ring. I will ask
the Rainforest creatures to organise
this."

Word was sent round the
Rainforest about the boxing match.
Some of the creatures were
summoned before the King and
instructed to build a boxing ring.
They trooped off to the clearing to
begin their task. Four wooden
posts were put into the ground that
marked out the ring. Spiders wove
a thick rope web around the posts
so that the boxers wouldn't fall out

of the ring. Everything was ready for the big fight.

CHAPTER 8

It was the night of the boxing match.

Before it was due to start, thousands of Rainforest creatures flocked in to support Stanley. All the giant monkey supporters turned up as well.

Shortly before the fight, the King visited Stanley in his dressing room.

"Good luck Stanley," said the King.

Stanley told the King he had nothing to worry about because he was confident he had the right tactics to win the fight.

It was time for the fighters to leave their dressing rooms. A great cheer went up as Stanley and the giant monkey made their way through the crowd and climbed into the ring. The King noticed that whilst the monkey had boxing gloves on both of his hands, Stanley had boxing gloves on all of his legs.

A scorpion made the announcement.

"Ladies and gentlecreatures, this fight is to decide who becomes King of the Rainforest. The one that lands a knockout blow will be the winner."

The bell sounded. Stanley and the giant monkey met in the centre of the ring. The fight began.

Within seconds, Stanley ran up the monkey's body and reached his face.

The last sounds the giant monkey heard before crashing to the floor

of the ring were the thump, thump,
thump, thump, thump, thump,
thump, thump of Stanley's eight
boxing gloved legs hitting him!
The giant monkey had been
knocked out in the first minute of

the fight. Stanley was declared the winner.

But Stanley had achieved a remarkable victory for the King and all the other Rainforest creatures. He was carried shoulder high back to the dressing room. King Jaguar came to see him. "Absolutely fantastic Stanley!" said the King. "Because of your victory, you are now a very special Rainforest creature. Please be my guest tomorrow at the palace and you can see something of what a King has to do."

Stanley accepted the invitation and the next morning, he made his way to the palace.

CHAPTER 9

Stanley arrived at the palace and was greeted by the King. "Come with me into my office Stanley. First job today is I have to meet with creatures who want to see me about various things, so you can sit in and see what goes on."
The King called out for the first creature to come into the office. The door opened and in came a snake.
"Good morning Mrs. Snake," said the King. "Have a seat and tell me the purpose of your visit."
"Thank you," said the snake. "Myself and a lot of other creatures I've talked to are getting tired of having to creep and crawl around the Rainforest looking for

food. We would like you to give us permission to build a supermarket so all the Rainforest creatures can come in and buy their prey, rather than having to rush out and catch it all the time."

"That's an interesting idea," said the King, "I'll give it some thought."

"Thank you," said the snake. She slithered her way out of the office. The King turned to Stanley. "What do you think of that idea?"

Stanley wanted to know where the snake got her ridiculous ideas from.

"It's usually when the Rainforest creatures' relatives from the cities come to visit. They tell them all about the things that are going on there. Perhaps the snake has got a point. It would make life a lot easier if creatures could go into a supermarket and buy freshly caught prey. Spiders like you could buy tinned flies instead of hanging around a web all day waiting to catch food," said the King.

"That's all very well," said Stanley. "But think of what would happen if you did open a supermarket. All the creatures would become fat and unhealthy because they wouldn't be getting the exercise of running around to catch food in the forest."

"Good point," said the King.

"Let's see what the next creature wants."

There was a knock at the door and in came a monkey.

"Good morning," said the King.

"Good morning, King Jaguar," said the monkey. "Good morning, Stanley. Well done last night. No hard feelings."

"What can I do for you today?" asked the King.

"I've been hearing from my friends who live at the edge of the Rainforest about men coming in and chopping lots of trees down. If this carries on, it's going to get a little crowded as the Rainforest gets smaller and smaller. Do you have any ideas as to what we should do about this?" asked the monkey.

"I've heard that this tree chopping is going on and it is a very serious problem. I will have to think of something very quickly to see if anything can be done," replied the King.

The monkey left the King's office. The King could not think of a plan that might save the Rainforest from the tree choppers but perhaps someone else could. He turned to Stanley and asked him if he would accept the very important job of saving the Rainforest.

Stanley thought about this.

"This could be an almost impossible task, but I might be able to come up with a plan," said Stanley.

"That sounds very encouraging," said the King.

"I'd better get on with it then!" said Stanley.

Stanley left the palace and made his way home.

CHAPTER 10

On his way home, Stanley passed
the clearing and saw the lady
spider looking after her kids as
usual.

"Hi lady spider, how's things?"
asked Stanley.

"Not too bad Stanley, I'm still
waiting for my husband to come
home from the carnival. What are
you up to?"

Stanley told her about being in the
King's office and the news that the
monkey had about how things
were getting really serious at the
edge of the Rainforest because of
men chopping lots of trees down.

"The King has given me the job of
trying to stop the tree choppers and
save the Rainforest," said Stanley.

"Sounds like a very difficult job Stanley," said the lady spider. "Certainly is," replied Stanley. "I'll have to come up with something though."

The days passed and Stanley tried very hard to think of something that would stop the trees of the Rainforest being chopped down but he could not think of an answer.

One day there was a knock on his web. It was the lady spider.

"Hi Stanley," she said, "I thought of an idea of how to stop the tree choppers! What if we built a wire fence around the forest and connected it up to the electric eels so anybody touching the fence would get a big electric shock!"

Stanley thought it was not a bad idea but he explained that all the tree choppers needed to do would be to drive a big truck over the fence and destroy it.

"Oh well," said the lady spider, "I can't think of anything else. Why not ask the wise old parrot who lives at the top of that large tree over there? He might be able to help."

"Good idea," said Stanley. "Nothing to lose. I'll make my way up there and see if he can give me any advice."

Stanley climbed his way up to the parrot's home at the top of the tree and introduced himself.

"Mr. Parrot, I am Stanley and I have been given the special task of saving the Rainforest from the tree

choppers. I have thought about
what to do but I have not yet come
up with any good ideas. I have
come to see you to ask your advice
on what I and my fellow
Rainforest creatures could do."
The wise old parrot spoke:
"You must be courageous and

fight the tree choppers or the Rainforest and its creatures will die.

Stanley, it is all a matter of numbers. How many tree choppers do you think come each time?"

"Probably not more than fifty," answered Stanley.

"Now how many soldier ants do you think there are in the Rainforest?" asked the parrot.

"Millions probably," replied Stanley.

"There you have it Stanley," said the parrot. "Millions of tiny ants can overcome fifty tree choppers! You know how brave and strong the soldier ants are when defending their own territory. You must tell them that the whole Rainforest is not only for them, it is also for all the other creatures that live and depend on it.

As the ants are the greatest in numbers, it is their duty to defend the Rainforest.

Stanley, you are the leader. It is you who must decide how the soldier ants can fight off the tree choppers.

Think out your tactics carefully and you will succeed."

Stanley thanked the wise old parrot and climbed down the tree. On his way back to his web, Stanley was thinking about how the soldier ants could defeat the tree choppers.

By the time he had reached his home, Stanley had thought up a plan of action.

CHAPTER 11

Stanley went to see his friend the ant and told him what the wise old parrot had to say.

"We need to train the soldier ants on how to repel the tree choppers," said Stanley.

Stanley told the ant about his secret plan.

"Sounds like a good idea Stanley," said the ant. "I'll go and have a word with the other ants and tell them of your plan of action. Then we will send a messenger ant to tell the next group and so on, until all the Rainforest ants know what is expected of them."

"But what about training them for the battle?" asked Stanley.

"No need Stanley," replied the ant. "We soldier ants know how to successfully defend territory. All we need is the signal to attack. Remember the instructions on how to play the teapot and make it sound like a trumpet?"

Stanley said he remembered.

"Good," said the ant. "Learn how to play the teapot Stanley, so you will be able to sound the signal for attack!"

"Great idea!" said Stanley. "We will also need the Black Howler monkeys to be spread across the whole Rainforest as lookouts, so they can relay a signal of three whoops when the tree choppers come and where they can be found."

"What if the tree choppers come to a part of the forest that is a long distance away? How are you going to get over there quickly enough to sound the attack?" asked the ant.

"I know," said Stanley, "I'll have a word with a friendly toucan who could fly me over to where the tree choppers are."

"Brilliant!" said the ant. "Anything else to do that we haven't thought of?"

"No, I think that's it," said Stanley. "All I have to do now is practise playing the teapot, tell the monkeys what they have to do and make arrangements with the toucan. I need you to make sure the message goes out to all the soldier ants in the Rainforest. They must be ready to go into action

against the tree choppers when they hear a blast from the teapot." Stanley and the ant set off to do the work that needed to be done.
Now it was just a matter of time before the warning signal would come from the monkeys that the tree choppers had arrived.

CHAPTER 12

A few days later and just as
Stanley expected, there was a loud
three whoops from the monkeys.
Stanley called for the toucan to fly
down to the forest floor. Carrying
the teapot, he jumped onto the
back of the toucan and they took
off.

Soon they were flying high above the Rainforest.

Stanley heard the whoops of the monkeys
signalling where the tree choppers were. Stanley soon spotted them.

"Over there, to the left," shouted Stanley.

The toucan flew down to the forest floor and landed a few yards away from where the tree choppers were preparing to chop down the first trees of the day.

Stanley climbed off the toucan's back and blew three long blasts on the teapot – the signal for attack!

On hearing the signal,
thousands of soldier ants swarmed towards the tree choppers. The ants crawled all over them, covering

each one from head to toe and biting them all over their bodies. The tree choppers could not stand the ants biting them and they ran away to escape in their trucks. Before the tree choppers made their escape, the ants made their way back down the chopper's bodies onto the ground and ran triumphantly back into the Rainforest.

"We've done it! We've done it!" shouted the ants. "We've seen them off; they'll never come back again!"

The monkeys came down from the trees to congratulate the soldier ants on their victory.

Stanley was also very happy with the ants' achievement but he also felt that this might not be the end of the story. The tree choppers might come back and try again. Stanley warned the ants, who were preparing for a victory party, that the battle for the Rainforest might not be over. Stanley thought that he should stay with the ants to see what might happen the next day. The next morning, just as Stanley had predicted, the tree choppers returned. This time, Stanley noticed that they were all wearing protective suits. Stanley now had to decide how the ants could defeat the choppers again.

He gave instructions to the ants. "On the sound of the teapot, everyone is to climb up the protective suits and cover the visors which help the choppers see where they are going."

Stanley blew the signal for attack. As they had been instructed to do, the ants ran up the protective suits of the choppers and completely covered their visors so they couldn't see anything. The moment they brushed the ants off their visors to see again, more ants quickly covered the visors again, making it impossible for the tree choppers to continue any further. Once again, the tree choppers had to give up and return to their trucks.

The triumphant ants returned back into the Rainforest. Once again, the ants celebrated their success over the tree choppers and thought that would definitely be the end of things. But Stanley was still feeling a little cautious.

He spoke to the toucan. "Perhaps they may come back again and try something different to protect themselves from the ants?"

"You could be right Stanley," replied the toucan.

"I'd better tell the ants to be on their guard again tomorrow, just in case," said Stanley.

The next morning, just as Stanley had feared, he saw the tree choppers' trucks arrive. He called to the ants to prepare for battle once again.

But things were different this time. The tree choppers walked towards the Rainforest and Stanley noticed that this time they were not carrying their axes. The tree choppers stopped at the edge of the Rainforest and began to sing.

Creatures of the Rainforest we salute you,
You have defended your forest very well.
We will not chop down your trees,
You've brought us to our knees,
We'll never ever bother you again!

The tree choppers turned around, went back to their trucks and drove off.

All the ants cheered, the monkeys screamed, the birds sang. Stanley and the soldier ants had saved the Rainforest! Stanley thanked the ants for their bravery. He called over to the toucan, climbed aboard and they flew back to their area of the Rainforest.

CHAPTER 13

Before Stanley had returned, word
had spread through the Rainforest
that Stanley and the ants had
beaten the tree choppers. A large
welcoming party led by the King
waited to greet Stanley as he
touched down.

There was a great cheer as Stanley
climbed down off the toucan.

"Well done Stanley!" said the
King. "You have achieved
something really magnificent!"

"Thank you King Jaguar," said
Stanley. "I may have planned the
defence of the Rainforest but the
battle was won by the soldier ants,
who were very brave, and let's not
forget the help of the monkeys

who sounded the alarm. It was all down to good team work!"

"Thank you for that Stanley," said the King. "We should have a big celebration and have the ants as our special guests. What do you think iguana?"

"We know all about Stanley's fantastic guitar playing. How about asking Stanley to form a band and we could have a massive celebration concert!" replied the iguana.

"What do you think Stanley?" asked the King.

"I suppose I could make some more guitars and have a few more spiders learn how to play," said Stanley.

"Good," said the King. "We'll have the concert a week today and

I'm sure that we will all have a great time."

After all the fuss had died down, Stanley was making his way home, when he passed the clearing where he saw the lady spider once again looking after her kids. Stanley went over to her.

"Hello lady spider," he said. "Still on your own?"

"Got a bit of bad news Stanley," she replied. "My husband's friend the tarantula came back from the carnival alone. He told me that my husband had met another lady spider in Rio and he has gone off with her. Now I am all alone with five hundred kids to feed and look after."

"I'm very sorry to hear that," said Stanley.

"I suppose that's the way things go," said the lady spider.

What the lady spider did not know was that Stanley had always liked her and he decided that she needed a good husband to look after her and the kids.

"I'm thinking of taking things a bit easier now that the Rainforest is safe. How would you like to have me as your new husband?" asked Stanley.

What Stanley did not know was that the lady spider thought Stanley was not only a very special spider, but that he was also really good-looking and had a lovely smile.

It took her less than a second before replying 'yes' to Stanley's offer of marriage. Stanley was overjoyed on hearing her reply. But now he had to think about the big concert and hoped that he and the other spiders in the band would give the performance of their lives.

CHAPTER 14

The ant had already organised the
making of two more guitars, two
more amplifiers and had also made
a drum kit. Stanley came along to
see how things were going.
"Everything is going well," said
the ant. "I've found a spider
drummer, a spider rhythm guitarist
and a spider bass guitarist and they
have been practising every day to
be ready for the concert."
"Sounds good," said Stanley.
"What do you think we should call
the band?"
"Sorted that one out as well,
Stanley," said the ant. He showed
Stanley the bass drum that had

STANLEY
AND
THE SPIDERS

painted on the front of it.

"Fantastic!" said Stanley.

"Don't worry, Stanley," said the ant, "everything is under control. I've sorted out the stage, the lighting, the lot. All you need to do now is have plenty of rehearsal time with the other members of the band to make sure you give a good performance on the night."

The night of the performance came. Everything had been prepared. The stage was a large branch. The stage lighting was a single light bulb powered by one of the electric eels.

A huge and excited crowd gathered in the clearing, waiting to see Stanley and the Spiders. As they were special guests, the soldier ants were given front row seats.

It was time for Stanley and his band to take to the stage.

As they arrived on stage, there was a huge cheer from the audience. Stanley made an announcement to the crowd:

"Hello everybody! We are Stanley and the Spiders."

The band opened up with 'Incy Wincy Spider' and the crowd went absolutely wild.

One hour later, the concert was over. Everybody had a great time. As Stanley left the stage, he was greeted by his wife-to-be.

"What a performance Stanley!"
she said. "Let's go home now
because I'd like to give you a great
big hug!"
"That's wonderful," said Stanley.
"Your web or mine?"

VISIT STANLEY'S WEBSITE
www.noahsrocket.com

WATCH STANLEY
AND THE SPIDERS
PERFORM
INCY WINCY SPIDER